Dear Parents and Educators,

Welcome to Penguin Young Readers! As parents and educators, you know that each child develops at his or her own pace—in terms of speech, critical thinking, and, of course, reading. Penguin Young Readers recognizes this fact. As a result, each Penguin Young Readers book is assigned a traditional easy-to-read level (1–4) as well as a Guided Reading Level (A–P). Both of these systems will help you choose the right book for your child. Please refer to the back of each book for specific leveling information. Penguin Young Readers features esteemed authors and illustrators, stories about favorite characters, fascinating nonfiction, and more!

Peter Rabbit™: I Am Benjamin

LEVEL **2**

GUIDED READING LEVEL **G**

This book is perfect for a **Progressing Reader** who:
- can figure out unknown words by using picture and context clues;
- can recognize beginning, middle, and ending sounds;
- can make and confirm predictions about what will happen in the text; and
- can distinguish between fiction and nonfiction.

Here are some **activities** you can do during and after reading this book:
- Read the Pictures: Use the pictures to tell the story. Have the child go through the book, retelling the story just by looking at the pictures.
- Character Traits: One of Benjamin Bunny's character traits is that he is funny. Write a list of some of his other trai[t]s.

Remember, sharing the love of reading wi[th] you can give!

D0955063

—Bonnie Bader, EdM
   Penguin Young Readers program

*Penguin Young Readers are leveled by independent reviewers applying the standards developed by Irene Fountas and Gay Su Pinnell in *Matching Books to Readers: Using Leveled Books in Guided Reading*, Heinemann, 1999.

PENGUIN YOUNG READERS
Published by the Penguin Group
Penguin Group (USA) LLC, 375 Hudson Street, New York, New York 10014, USA

USA | Canada | UK | Ireland | Australia | New Zealand | India | South Africa | China

penguin.com
A Penguin Random House Company

Published by Penguin Young Readers, an imprint of Penguin Group (USA) LLC, 345 Hudson Street,
New York, New York 10014. Manufactured in China.

Library of Congress Cataloging-in-Publication Data is available.

ISBN 978-0-14-135746-1 (pbk)   10 9 8 7 6 5 4 3 2 1
ISBN 978-0-14-135745-4 (hc)   10 9 8 7 6 5 4 3 2 1

I Am Benjamin

Penguin Young Readers
An Imprint of Penguin Group (USA) LLC

I am Benjamin.

Benjamin Bunny.

Peter is my best friend.

Lily is my best friend, too.

Sometimes I can be clumsy.

Peter and Lily think I am funny.

Peter likes the garden.

There are a lot of good things

to eat there.

But it is also scary.

Peter wants Lily and me to come
to the garden, too.
"Are you sure this is
a good idea?" I ask.
"Yes," Peter says.

I run with Peter and Lily.

I get scared easily.

I tell myself, "Rabbits are brave.

Rabbits are brave."

We hear a noise.

Is it a cat?

No, it is my tummy!

"Sorry," I tell Peter and Lily.

"I am hungry."

We hear another noise.

This time it is not my tummy.

It is the badger, Tommy Brock.

And he is after Peter!

"This is bad.

This is really bad," I tell Lily.

"We have to help Peter!"

Lily and I run back to

the garden.

Lily jumps into a big boot.

I jump into a big boot.

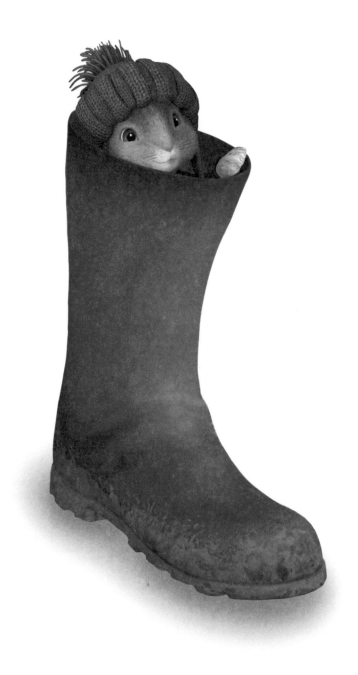

We look like a big man walking.

I call out in a deep voice,

"I do not like rabbits.

But I **really** do not like

smelly badgers!"

Tommy Brock is scared.

Peter is scared, too.

They think we are Mr. McGregor.

Tommy Brock drops Peter

and runs away.

But then Lily pops out

of her boot.

I pop out of my boot.

Peter is happy to see us.

We saved the day.

Then I hear something.

"Help, help!

It is after me!" I yell.

But it is only a snail.

Peter and Lily laugh.

I am Benjamin Bunny.

I am funny.

And a bit clumsy.

Sometimes I am scared.

But I am always a good friend!